Ruby Hastings
Writes Her Own Story

Written by Rachel Charlton-Dailey

Illustrated by Betsy Falco

Collins

Chapter 1

The words glare back at me in angry red pen. The word "any" is in capital letters and underlined twice so it's almost shouting at me.

My amazing story, that I worked so hard on all weekend, is now covered in ugly red crosses and circles by my teacher, Mr Atley.

For homework, we were asked to write about something that happened over the weekend and make the story exciting, so I wrote in my favourite style – a newspaper article.

MR ATLEY

ELSIE

JASPER

But now you can't even see how hard I worked on writing about my next door neighbour Elsie's missing cat, and the reward that was offered.

No, my teacher didn't read any of that, because apparently, he *couldn't*.

Mr Atley's always going on at me for my handwriting being too messy or smudged or the words being in the wrong order. I really tried with this though. It took ages and my hand was aching by the time I was done.

Mr Atley also always tells me off for butting in or doing things a little bit differently to everyone else. All these things are not my fault and he knows that.

I should probably tell you why none of this is my fault so you understand the rest of my story. My name is Ruby Hastings, I'm eleven and I'm dyspraxic.

Dyspraxia means my brain is wired differently to other people's. It affects how I move, talk and do things. It means I fall over a lot and have trouble with using things, especially small things like pens and pencils.

Other things dyspraxic people like me can't do very well:

◆ ride a bike (or any sports really)

◆ be on time; I'm always late

◆ follow instructions, but maybe if they're explained well I can

◆ keep up with conversations. I'm either lagging behind or jumping in. I also get called "blunt" or "rude" but I'm just telling people what I think

and finally

◆ dyspraxic people have terrible handwriting.

OK, the doctors and people who know things don't say "terrible", but I do, and so does Mr Atley.

The others aren't as important to me. If I'm a little bit late, at least I miss the awkward start of the chat that I can never see the point of. Also, who cares about PE anyway? Well Tam does, but not me. But writing is my life, *I mean it.*

When I grow up, I want to be a writer. Well, a journalist, just like my idol Susie Starling. Susie writes for a big newspaper, the *Daily Echo*. Everyone reads it, even Elsie.

PRESS
SUSIE STARLING

Susie talks to disabled people just like me because she's disabled too. She fights for our rights to live like everybody else. She's not afraid to stand up for what she believes, no matter who gets angry with her, even the Prime Minister, and that's a really important person, apparently.

REALLY IMPORTANT PERSON?

That's what I want to do. I want to make a difference. Except nobody can read what I write.

Tam cuts into my sulking. "I didn't even get to read this one!" she shouts, picking up my homework.

Tam's my best friend in the entire world. I love her nearly as much as my sister Ella. Tam and I knew we were going to be friends forever when some kids wouldn't let us play basketball with them at the local park.

No one wanted me to join their team because I can't catch, and they just assume Tam isn't good at sports because she uses a stick, walker or wheelchair, depending on how her body feels.

They're nearly always proved wrong though, as Tam can go faster than anyone else in her chair and land a throw from super faraway.

Tam wants to be a professional wheelchair basketball player when she grows up, like the ones we saw at the Paralympics. Those players are seriously tough – just like Tam.

"Well, he's right – I can't read it, but only 'cos he's scribbled all over it. Here, have this." Tam digs a chocolate bar out of the basket on her walker and presses it into my hand.

"Thanks, so now I'm guilty of eating your snacks, which you're not supposed to have in school." I roll my eyes but eat it anyway.

"If I'm getting into trouble, so are you," Tam laughs, raising her chocolate bar up to tap mine.

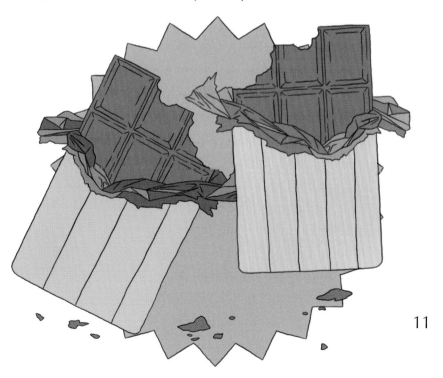

Chapter 2

Despite the chocolate bar, I'm still feeling grumpy about my homework at teatime.

"What's wrong, petal?" Aunty Beth asks, seeing my sad face. Aunty Beth looks after me when Dad's working at the hospital.

"Nothing," I reply, annoyed.

"Well, it sure looks like something."

She's got me there. I don't answer her; instead I hunch over further to read the newspaper.

"Got anything to do with that red pen mess all over your homework?" Ella asks. She's currently taking everything out of my schoolbag. Sometimes she knows me too well.

"What are you doing in my bag?"

"I couldn't find my scrunchie and I had a feeling where I'd find it – aha!" she shouts, pulling it out while still holding my homework.

"What red pen mess?" Aunty Beth asks, as Ella passes my homework to her. "Aw, love. I know you tried so hard with this one," she sighs.

"I really did! But now I'll never be a journalist like Susie Starling!" I huff.

"The stories you write are much more important than *how* you write," Ella tells me wisely.

"Not if nobody can read them!" I shout back.

"I'm pretty sure Saint Susie types all her columns on a computer," Ella points out.

"You've got natural talent when it comes to this. Your work will change the world one day." Aunty Beth smiles, and wraps me in a cuddle.

I know deep down they're right, but I still need to prove how good I am.

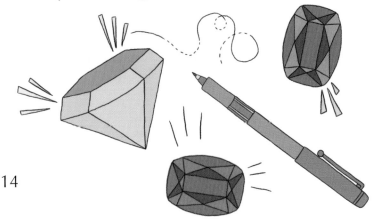

Tuesdays are usually my favourite days at school. This is for two reasons.

1 We do art on Tuesday.

2 It's taught by my favourite teacher, Miss Smiles.

Miss Smiles wears bright cardigans, and she lives up to her name. But today I don't want to paint as I'm worried Miss Smiles will think I'm bad at it.

"Please try and focus on the colours of the flowers, but you can paint the pot however you want. Express yourselves!" Miss Smiles tells us all as she wanders between the tables. She stops next to me and Tam. I try my best to cover my work but the paint is wet.

"I don't want you to look, you'll think it's terrible," I say quietly.

"What? Why would I ever think that?" she gasps.

I show her hesitantly. As she studies it, her smile gets bigger and bigger.

16

"This is wonderful! Look at those beautiful pinks
and reds. How are you going to decorate the pot?"
Miss Smiles asks.

I look over and see that Tam has painted hers blue with
pink and yellow spots, just like Miss Smiles' cardigan.

Miss Smiles grabs a spare flower and tucks it behind
her ear. When I don't smile, she looks worried but doesn't
say anything.

"Mr Atley crossed out all of Ruby's latest story so she thinks she'll never be Susie Starling," Tam tells her.

"But you're an amazing writer, you know that!" Miss Smiles tells me.

I shake my head.

"In fact, I've seen something that you'll love." Miss Smiles picks up a leaflet from her desk and presents it to me with a "Ta-dahh!"

I stare in shock: there's a new school newspaper. Even better, the first meeting is this lunch time. I have to join it!

SCHOOL NEWSPAPER

Writers and artists wanted.

Come to the library this Tuesday

lunch time to find out more!

I finish my lunch super fast and rush to the library.

"Woah, Speedy, you almost ran me over! What are you doing here?" Ella asks, shifting the library books in her arms. Did I mention Ella works in the school library?

I shove the leaflet at her, shouting, "This!"

Her eyes go really big, and she gets out of the way so I can see the table where the newspaper meeting is happening.

Oh no. This isn't good.

Chapter 3

Mr Atley's the teacher helping to run the paper. I'm never getting in the newspaper now.

Around the table there are some kids from my class and some from the year below. I take a seat next to Tam's brother, Jay.

"Thank you all for taking an interest in this," says Mr Atley. "I'm very excited for the school to have a newspaper. This is for the pupils, by the pupils. So, without further ado, over to our editor, Amelia Jenkins."

This is no surprise. Amelia's the most popular girl in school. Everyone loves her, especially the teachers.

Amelia explains that she wants the paper to be as crammed full of stories about the school and pupils as possible.

"Sounds great – I have *so* many ideas!" I say.

"Ruby, I'm just worried that you won't be able to keep up with the fast-paced environment without getting upset," Mr Atley says.

Ella's returning books to the shelves nearby. I hear her tut.

"Journalism is my life! I write news stories all the time!" I say.

"Yes, but we can't read any of it." Amelia echoes what Mr Atley said about my homework.

I need to think fast – oh wait! "I can do what Susie Starling does."

"Who?" Amelia asks.

"You don't know Susie Starling? She's an absolutely amazing journalist who writes about disabled people and stands up for everyone." I speak quickly and I can hear Amelia's friends snigger.

"And what does she do?" Amelia asks, sounding bored.

"She types them all!" I practically shout. "On her computer. I can do that, then Dad can email them to the school or I can print them out," I suggest, trying my best to convince everyone.

"Why don't you have a mix of half-written and half-typed stories in the paper?" Ella suggests.

"I can do drawings!" Jay shouts, excited.

Ella stares Mr Atley in the eye.

"I might like it …" Amelia says, sounding unsure.

"Fine!" Mr Atley sighs.

Yes! I'm going to be a journalist!

Chapter 4

"Dad, can I use the laptop?" I ask.

"Of course, darling. What are you up to?"

Dad's heated up Aunty Beth's vegetable soup and he's sneaking spoonfuls straight from the pan.

"Will you get a bowl?!" Aunty Beth says as she walks into the kitchen.

Dad wrinkles his nose at me and grabs a bowl.

"The school's started a newspaper; I'm a journalist now! This is all of my important research and stories," I explain, "but because my handwriting's bad, Mr Atley's letting me type mine out."

"Oh, that's good," Dad says.

"Yes, but I have so much to do before tomorrow!"

The next day, I rush into the library with my folder of
story plans and a couple of stories I typed up last night.
I've got so many ideas, especially about the disabled people
I know at school, like Annie who's blind. Maybe I can have
my own column! I can't keep my excitement in. Amelia is
mid speech when I dump my folder down on the table
before my arms give up.

"What's all this, Ruby? I was talking." She seems angry.

I start explaining about the different things I've written.

Mr Atley looks through the pages quickly while Amelia takes longer to read, sounding out the words.

"Well, there are so many mistakes in this, I wouldn't include it. But it's not my decision," says Mr Atley.

Amelia immediately puts my stories down, looking nervous. "I'm sorry, Ruby, I can barely read it."

I feel like I've just been prickled by nettles. It's typed out; I don't understand why she can't read it.

"I can try harder. Let me do some more for our next meeting," I say, putting my ideas back in the folder.

"Are you still writing?" Dad asks. He's just come in from work.

I need to make sure I've got enough to show Amelia tomorrow, but it's taking longer than I thought. I have to type slowly and make sure there are fewer mistakes.

"This seems like a lot, Rubes," Dad says. "Are you sure this isn't too much for you?"

"I NEED to do this," I groan.

"OK, OK, I'm just worried about you, as always."

"If she says she can do this, she can do it," Ella shrugs.

Ella's right. I *can*!

Finally, today's the day! The school newspaper is out! I'm so excited I drag Tam to the library before class starts. People are finally going to read what I write and learn so much about disabled people at school.

"Ruby, wait!" Tam laughs, narrowly avoiding people with her wheelchair.

"Tam, this is the biggest day of my life!" I shout, grabbing a paper. I leaf through, excited, trying to find my work.

Where is it?

Chapter 5

I can't believe it! Not one of my stories is in the paper.
I read it from front to back and back again, just to be sure.
How can this be? As I slam the paper down on my desk,
I see Amelia with her friends.

"Amelia! I need to talk to you NOW!" I shout, barging
into her conversation.

She grabs my arm and pulls me away.

"Ruby! Why are you upset now? Is this about the paper?" Amelia asks.

"Of course it's about the paper! Where are my stories?" I ask, getting upset.

"Ruby, they were full of spelling mistakes and took forever to get to the good bit. Nobody cares about Tam wanting to play basketball, or Annie's dog."

"Tam and Annie are incredible. They're funny and kind and creative, unlike you!" I'm really shouting now.

"They're RIDICULOUS and so are you, and no one wants to hear about your precious Susie Starling either!" Amelia shouts back.

That does it. I grab the paper she's holding and rip it to shreds.

Mr Atley would have to be walking by at that moment. "Ruby Hastings, what do you think you're doing?"

"Ruby screamed in my face and ripped up my newspaper!" Amelia wails.

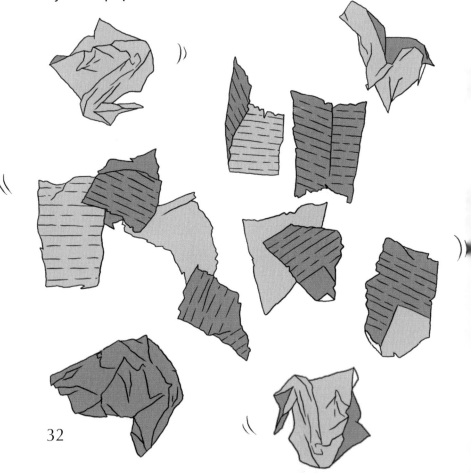

"Amelia didn't put any of my stories in the paper!" I tell Mr Atley.

"You destroyed the paper so many people worked so hard on," Amelia replies.

"I WORKED HARD." I grab the pile on the desk and dump them in the bin.

Chapter 6

Mr Atley makes me stay inside at lunch time, but when I get to the classroom, Miss Smiles is setting up for art.

"Hello, Ruby. It's such a lovely day, what are you doing here?"

"Mr Atley said I have to sit in here. I got angry and dumped the newspapers in a bin, but it was Amelia's fault." I try not to get upset again.

"Oh yes, I did hear about that," Miss Smiles sighs.

"I understand why you're upset, but I can see why Mr Atley's not happy." Miss Smiles starts putting the paint pots out.

"I worked *so* hard. I love writing but I get words mixed up and wrong. Maybe I'm just bad at it." I try to help Miss Smiles, but I knock over a pot of bright orange paint. "See, I can't do anything!"

"Just because you do things differently, it doesn't make them wrong," Miss Smiles tells me. "But destroying other people's work isn't the right way to show that."

I put my head down.

"What do I always tell you to do when you're feeling angry?" she reminds me.

"To stop, breathe and think about how I'm feeling before snapping," I sigh.

Tam and Jay are coming to mine for tea, so Ella walks us all home after school.

Aunty Beth's waiting for us. "What's this about you fighting? I had your teacher on the phone."

"I wasn't fighting! None of my stories were put in the paper," I say.

"They didn't put my drawings in either," Jay admits.

"You should campaign," Ella suggests. "Get people's attention – that might help people understand, more than binning the newspapers," she says.

"We could make posters!" Tam says.

"I feel like I should be warning you about getting into trouble," Aunty Beth sighs.

"Are you though?" Ella asks.

"Not when I think you're doing the right thing," she smiles.

A PAPER FOR EVERYONE

All stories diserve to be in the paper

I write "A PAPER FOR EVERYONE" in big letters on a large piece of paper. Tam adds some glitter stars and Jay starts to doodle lots of different people on the bottom.

"And that's your campaign," Ella smiles.

The next day we put up the posters at school. Ella's even going to take one to the headteacher.

As I'm sticking the last one on our classroom door, I hear a phone camera noise. I spin around to see Ella smiling.

"I'm so proud of you! Can I post this online?" she asks. I nod, excited. She hugs me again and rushes off to the library.

As everyone starts to pile into the classroom, they all stop and stare at the poster.

"MR ATLEY!" Amelia shrieks.

Mr Atley looks at the poster. "I've got a feeling I know who did this. Ruby Hastings, come here," he orders.

I try to stand as tall as I can and not show my nerves.

"Can you explain this?" He points to the poster.

"Everyone deserves to be in the newspaper. It's wrong not to include work because people write differently."
I force myself to look him in the eye.

"I'm sure this took you a very long time, but the paper is out now," Mr Atley says.

"Well then, the next issue," I push.

"You've proved you don't deserve to be in the paper," Amelia huffs.

"EVERYONE deserves to be in the paper!" I shout.

"That's enough, Amelia's the editor. Go to your seats now!" Mr Atley says.

40

When the bell finally goes, Tam and I rush out, but Ella grabs us as we go past the library.

"Ruby! You've got to see this!"

She sits me down in front of the computer and opens the site for the newspaper that Susie Starling writes for.

"See that?" Ella points.

I don't believe this. Susie Starling has written about me!

Chapter 7

It's right in front of me and I still can't believe it's real.
Susie Starling not only knows who I am, but she's written
a story about ME. She calls me "super brave" and says that
I'm "standing up for what's right".

Ella explains that the photo of me she posted online was super popular. Then Susie sent Ella a message to find out about the campaign and ask if she could write about it.

"That's not all. Susie's asked if she can meet you when she's back in town on Saturday," Ella reveals.

I try my best not to scream but my brain can't take it.

I can't believe Susie Starling's in my house, sitting at my kitchen table, drinking tea and eating Aunty Beth's flapjacks. She's just chatting to my family like she isn't a megastar, while I sit opening and closing my mouth like a fish.

"I was so impressed with your campaign, Ruby. That took real guts," she tells me.

I almost choke on my juice.

"Thank you," I squeak. "What *you* do takes real courage though, all the people you stand up to. I want to be like you, but I can't," I sigh.

"Why not? Your work is good and you have a big heart," Susie says.

"Wait, you've read my work?" Ella looks guilty, so I know she sent it to Susie. I throw her a look.

"Hey, I'm glad she showed me. I'd love to see what you do in the future," Susie smiles.

"Well, there won't be any in the future; my stupid dyspraxia has put an end to that."

"It didn't stop me," Susie says.

My mouth opens wide in shock. "You're dyspraxic?" I say quietly, so that only Susie can hear me. She nods.

"But you're a real journalist, you interview important people and you're so cool!" I gasp.

"I work to my strengths. I might be late a lot, but I work really well under stress. OK, so I jump in on conversations and people might think I'm rude – but I get to the root of what matters and get the important details," she explains.

"How can you do all of this with dyspraxia?"
I ask, confused.

"I have to double- and triple-check my work and I have
editors who do that too. I work to my own timetable and
I'm not hard on myself. That's what you need to do too."

I hear what Susie's saying but it just doesn't feel possible. I'm almost in tears when she leans over to touch my hand.

"You're going to do amazing things, Ruby, but you need to believe in and be kind to yourself."

"But I'm never going to be allowed back on the newspaper now," I sniffle.

"When people told me disabled people's stories weren't important, I published them myself." Susie looks at me.

That's it! "I can start my own paper!"

Susie holds up my poster. "*Everyone* deserves a paper."

Chapter 8

After my chat with Susie, life seemed to go into super speed. I've barely had time to sit down.

Susie helped me make a big list of what I wanted the paper to be:

- a paper for disabled kids and teens, *by* disabled kids and teens

- tell our stories our way, without us having to be amazing or sad

- pictures, photos and everything else by disabled kids and teens too – because stories can be told in lots of ways.

We had a video call meeting with some important people at Susie's paper a couple of days after I met Susie. I was shaking with fear, but Susie said I pitched the idea to them really well.

I couldn't believe my ears when they asked if they could publish it, with me as editor and Susie helping me.

ME, a newspaper editor!

Next, I had to find kids to write for it. I put posters in the library and Ella and Susie sent a call out to other local schools.

We named the paper *For Everyone*, because everybody deserves to see themselves and people like them in newspapers, books and everything else.

Tonight is the launch party. I know I say this a lot, but I can't believe this is happening.

We're having the party where it all began: in the school library. Ella's decorated it with colourful banners and posters made by Tam and Jay. As I look around the room, I'm so proud of what I've made happen.

"Ruby, this is amazing!" Amelia breaks me out of my daze by hugging me. "I'm sorry for not including you in the school paper but thank you for letting me be a part of yours," she smiles.

To be honest I didn't want to, but then I read what she'd written to us and knew I had to.

Hi Ruby and Susie

I know you will probly delete this but I was wondernig if I could write about how hard it is being a writer when my brian jumbles up words and letters. Ruby I'm so sorry.
Amelia

Amelia's learnt to be proud of having dyslexia and I've made her my deputy editor. Like me, what she says is more important than how she writes.

Ella rushes over and hands me her phone. "I've got someone who wants to speak to you!"

"It's Ruby Hastings, editor of *For Everyone*!" Susie cheers.

"Hi, Susie! Aren't you interviewing the new Prime Minister or something?"

"Ahh, you're more important!"

I make a noise that tells her I doubt that.

"I wish you were here," I admit.

"Me too, I'm so proud of you. You're an incredible writer, which is why, when I'm on holiday next month, I suggested to my editor that you write my column instead."

"WHAT?" I shout.

Susie smiles. "My editor already said yes. What do you say?"

"Ruby Hastings, columnist at the *Daily Echo*," I laugh. "I say, YES!"

I always thought my condition was the reason I couldn't be a journalist, but Susie has shown me that dyspraxia makes us both who we are.

And I love being me.

Ruby Hastings discovers her strengths

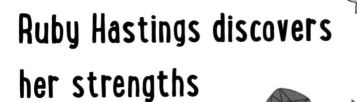

loyal

determined

blunt (not a bad thing!)

passionate

54

creative

focused

stands up for what's right

community-minded

What are YOUR strengths?

Ideas for reading

Written by Christine Whitney
Primary Literacy Consultant

Reading objectives:
- check that the book makes sense to them, discussing their understanding and exploring the meaning of words in context
- draw inferences such as inferring characters' feelings, thoughts and motives from their actions
- predict what might happen from details stated and implied
- summarise the main ideas drawn from more than one paragraph, identifying key details that support the main ideas
- identify and discuss themes in a wide range of writing
- provide reasoned justifications for their views

Spoken language objectives:
- participate in discussions
- use spoken language to develop understanding through speculating, hypothesising, imagining and exploring ideas
- ask relevant questions

Curriculum links: PSHE education – learn to recognise the ways in which they are the same and different to others

Interest words: dyspraxic, disabled, dyslexia, campaign

Build a context for reading
- Before looking at the book, encourage children to discuss what they would write about if they were a writer.
- Ask the children if they have heard the words *dyslexia* and *dyspraxia*, and ask them to explain their understanding of these. Definitions may need to be provided.
- Look at the title on the front cover, then closely at the illustration. With knowledge of the previous words from question 2, discuss what this story might be about. Look together at the back cover and ask children to add to their predictions. What could be Ruby's story?

Understand and apply reading strategies
- Read Chapter 1 together. Summarise what the reader knows about Ruby by the end of the chapter.
- Continue to read together up to the end of Chapter 2. Ask children to explain why Ruby stares *in shock* at the leaflet Miss Smiles presents to her.